A.V.T.A. Life

Cinque T. Lee

authorHOUSE

AuthorHouse™
1663 Liberty Drive
Bloomington, IN 47403
www.authorhouse.com
Phone: 833-262-8899

Published by AuthorHouse 07/07/2022

ISBN: 978-1-6655-5617-0 (sc)
ISBN: 978-1-6655-5629-3 (e)

Definition - "A.V.T.A." - Created by Scammers
V.V.'s - Virtual Versions
<u>Advanced •Virtual • Technology</u>

<u>• Activation</u>

- Life is the first option

- Death is the second option

- A.V.T.A. is the third option

- The Judge - Judge Butler

It explains what the world has come to in the year 2050. The planet has become totally controlled by scammers who have gotten so wealthy that they are unstoppable. Actually these scammers have the power to live on a planet that hasn't been discovered yet. "V.V." meaning Virtual Version is what has made the scammers so rich and powerful.

People are always hurt and very desperate after the death of a loved one. For example, when a husband loses his wife, he is immediately contacted by scammers who take advantage of his pain and offers him the choice of having his wife back with V.V. so that he can have the virtual version of his wife to live with him. It is very expensive costing $ 2,000 for the down payment and $ 7,000 per year. The scammers are in total control of this technology and they have the world in mercy and law authorities are lost and are also customers of these scammers. A.V.T.A. was created in 2049 by scammers worldwide putting their technology together not only for money but for power.

"A.V.T.A. Life"

Life

Death

A.V. T. A

The purchaser of each V.V. must not lose focus of reality or else it all becomes deadly. Each V.V. can only be physically touched three times, they seem so real and better than the deceased person. So many people forget that it isn't real and try to touch it but that is the wrong move. The V.V. must not be touched more than three times or it will murder the person who bought it and have rights to the property and assets of that person, it is written in the contracts of each V.V. The contracts are twenty pages long and are not fully read and understood because the person buying V.V. is in so much pain and very, very anxious to have their loved ones back as soon as possible. A receipt or contract is constantly overlooked. Many people want to repair many damaged relationships now that there is another chance. The children and women are the ones mostly made into victims but men are extremely lost too because anger and control always make them forget about reality especially when the V.V.'s have perfect behavior and look like a younger version of his wife. Each contract also states that all children must not be in contact with the V.V. because kids always want to hug their parents. The V.V.'s might seem to show love and affection but they do not have any feelings at all. They are controlled by scammers who are mostly after the valuables of the person who purchased it.

The scammers maintain control of all V.V.'s even after they're bought. Agreements were reached by the government and the scammers allowing them access to rockets used by astronauts as long as each person is given three chances to live when a V.V. is touched physically, with high numbers of new customers daily, the scammers became rich in weeks. The government had to satisfy the scammers or else there would be more deaths. When a person touches the V.V. three times, control is automatically given back to the scammers who've acquired all information of what is worth money like houses, vehicles, and bank accounts. If a payment is missed it will also give complete control of the V.V. to the scammers. The V.V. will then take ownership of the properties and allowed to live on its own wherever is chosen by the scammers.

The scammers went to into space at least three times a week. With many astronauts at the control of the scammers it helped them to find a planet that wasn't discovered yet. On this new planet, people are able live there like on Earth. The scammers quickly left Earth when they noticed that controlling the V.V. isn't difficult at all on this new planet. They would constantly bring their friends and relatives to live with them on this planet and leave Earth behind as the V.V.'s population rose rapidly everyday.

Most of the scammers feel untouchable and often murder before it gets touched three times, just to speed up the process of scammers taking ownership of what was owned by a person. In these contracts it also states that if the V.V. kills before being touched three times, the scammers are required to return two of their friends or relatives back to Earth and face incarceration for ten years at least, depending on the number of people it killed. That V.V. would have to then be deactivated by the scammers. If the scammers don't honor the agreement, the government will not give them access to the rockets. It will only bring more rage on both sides but the scammers always get the last laugh because they have numerous V.V.'s throughout every city in the whole world. Scammers have no clue about space and rockets so they greatly need the astronauts and the government to give them access to the rockets whenever requested. Another major goal of the scammers besides money and murder is to forever leave Earth where the F.B.I. can eventually capture the scammers and then bring them to justice. If any member of the F.B.I. purchases a V.V. then that officer will be jailed for twenty years. A high number of the F.B.I. agents secretly still buy a V.V. because the pain is overwhelming. Most of the scammers are willing to just wait because they see how much and how fast that A.V.T.A. has engulfed the world. For example, more than sixty percent of the natural deaths end with A.V.T.A. and as the numbers rise, the scammers get richer being able to hide on a new planet while their V.V.'s keep murdering. If never caught, the V.V. will live on Earth like it was a real person. Until the scammers are found, the only way to communicate with them is through computers.

Judge Greg Butler was one of the first two times that scammers offered A.V.T.A. He died from medical reasons at age sixty-one. His parents were shocked and scammers bought the third option of V.V. to them in a couple of hours while searching their financial records. They weren't concerned about the price because they were a wealthy couple. The parents didn't fully read through the contract. They both tried to hold and hug the V.V., and in three days, he killed them both. He refused to take their fortunes because the highest power, God, took control of the judge who helped many with justice.

A righteous person like Judge Butler would've never harmed his parents. The regret itself would tear him apart. His love for what is right and his love for his parents is too strong for the scammers and it shows that love is stronger than anything. Days later as he layed on the ground screaming "No, no!" He punches the ground as the rain pours down very hard. Then, thunder strikes him and tells him that he is the last judge left making him the last hope for the new world that has been hit with A.V.T.A. The law enforcement and military try to assist the judge in every way possible because the V.V.'s are really uncontrollable. This last court gets bombarded by hundreds of new V.V. cases every week.

An average judge cannot take so much stress. Though he is able to handle the majority of the cases, he isn't perfect. He has limits and those assisting him have to somehow work alot harder. All that Judge Butler can do is bring peace to hurt families and keep a close eye on A.V.T.A. He is able take cases 24 hours a day. He really hopes that he himself can be forgiven for what he did to his parents. The scammers realize that they no longer have control of the judge and despise him because they can't figure out why and how they just can't control him. He knows that it is his duty to prevent the V.V.'s from non-stop murders and help the children and other relatives of the deceased to get back on track.

When buying the V.V., the first two hours are for programming it. The person buying it will teach V.V.'s all of the habits of the person deceased. The V.V. will be complete and very similar within minutes after the programming.

Children and their mothers are the most victims of V.V.'s. Women are very sensitive and peaceful while kids aren't smart enough yet to realize what is really going on. Some children are spared depending on the attitude of the scammer at that time but most of them are held for ransom so that the scammers get what they want. If the child is who violated the contract then the child will meet the terrible fate along with the parent or whoever bought the V.V. Neither a man or a woman is strong enough against a V.V.

One day, Judge Butler has to decide a case that is similar to his own. The V.V. had killed his parents. This case hits the judge hard. The scammers released the V.V. to court awaiting to obtain the dead parents' properties. Judge Butler really wants to cry but he can't. He refuses to release the properties to the V.V. and it totally enrages the scammers to the point that neither the amount of V.V. related deaths had doubled. The judge is at a point where many people try to judge him. People are lost and afraid as they shout different opinions to the judge. All of the screams and the similarity of this case to his own causes the judge to fall down rolling back and forth while he screams "No, no!" The size of the judge would shrink in three minutes causing him to fall from over three hundred pounds to two hundred and twenty pounds as he rolled on the floor. When the judge fell down, it allowed scammers to get some control of him again. If the judge shrinks too much then he will vanish. If there is not a judge like him, then the world will go under. Many children and other family members of the people who have been killed by a V.V. will starve and become homeless. The scammers refuse to just simply delete a V.V. that has committed murder because they don't like

Cinque T. Lee

having to send their relatives back to Earth and all of the money they make from each purchase. There's still a large number of scammers who choose to remain on Earth due to alot of differences with other scammers and many want complete control of A.V.T.A. that's greed to the fullest. Many of the scammers believe that they will always have control of A.V.T.A. but as the number of V.V.'s quickly add up, once there is more V.V.'s than people, a major world war will immediately happen and then A.V.T.A. will rule the world. Any scammers remaining on Earth will meet the fate of the rest of the people on Earth. Many of the scammers don't realize it plus there are many scammers who just can't see eye to eye and work together because the large amounts of money coming so fast makes all of the scammers extremely greedy. All of the scammers on the new planet eventually run out of food and have to negotiate with the scammers remaining on Earth just to get food. All of the selfishness doesn't let the negotiating last more than two weeks. As the V.V.'s conquer Earth with the war, the large number of scammers left have no other choice than work with each other so that they can keep the small amount of control they have left because A.V.T.A. has become too major and too fast. It shows charma or when you commit something that is wrong, it will no doubt come back to haunt you. It also shows that righteousness will always reign supreme, like with Judge Butler, his true love for his parents totally back fired on the scammers. They never would have thought that one of the V.V.'s first created would be one of their obstacles down the line.

Once again, a storm hits hard. As the judge was rolling on the floor, thunder strikes him again. The judge looked up while he was still shrinking and shouting "No, no!" When the thunder struck him, he was quiet and frowning at his security who allowed the V.V. on trial to walk away untouched and very rich. The law enforcement is useless against a V.V. The judge stood up and lifted his arms up to the sky. Still quiet, he sat back in his seat, looking at his recent case files with so many empty spaces. He then looked at the next V.V. in his court. Though the judge has lost alot of weight, he hopes that the thunder would strike him again making him as strong as before. He doesn't know it, but the thunder won't strike again until there is more love everywhere. There is still alot of love on Earth, but A.V.T.A. is expanding rapidly.

Without Judge Butler, what will happen to Earth. There will be more homeless and starving people at the hands of A.V.T.A. There is going to be a war between the people and the scammers.

Alot of scammers will be at war with each other because controlling A.V.T.A. has really become too difficult for anyone. The scammers that are on the new planet have become more desperate to get food so their schemes have tripled. Just to get food, the scammers release more V.V.'s than they can handle and that gives the V.V.'s more control. The V.V.'s do not have feelings at all. Their first concern is money and the other is murder. With the A.V.T.A. population catching up to the human population and more than half of people are still living with the V.V.'s because being hurt and hit with the pain of losing someone that is so close to them, will often cause them to lose focus, and forget about reality. The V.V.'s notice the pain and weakness so they only aim to take advantage of many. People really have to come to their senses. It seems that alot of people have lost hope in their religions and devote the

Cinque T. Lee

most of their time and money to the scammers with A.V.T.A. and that alone has caused the government to lose their control and must only satisfy the requests of the scammers who don't even have full control of what they've created.

Can people finally come together, show love to each other and unite against A.V.T.A. If the real love isn't displayed, the thunder won't strike again. The thunder is really the voice from heaven. If the thunder doesn't strike Judge Butler and give him the force that he needs to maintain the small things that people have left. Police and military already have their hands full dealing with crime and terrorism. A.V.T.A. is being purchased by them also. The judge is really all that Earth has left. Only the judge knows that he will vanish if the world doesn't display more love and understand that there are only two options, life and death. People are indeed very happy that when the judge fell, he was able to stand again and provide some justice when V.V.'s are out of control. Many presidents from different countries were in tears and fell down screaming themselves when they thought that the judge was no more. The majority of the world feels that A.V.T.A. is helpful, because so many are happy again because of V.V. Alot of people don't even care about their money or property. Alot of people even put A.V.T.A. over their remaining family members, even children. That shows how blind people have become.

Many of the scammers do realize that controlling A.V.T.A. is quickly decreasing. The scammers are just to afraid to go against A.V.T.A. The scammers are cowards anyway and charma is effecting them. When a person does wrong, it will definitely come back to haunt them. This is why alot of scammers are against each other and the rest of them are basically stranded on another planet and their food supply is getting smaller. The big plot of A.V.T.A. has backfired on them.

A large number of scammers choose not to accept the fact that A.V.T.A. has really become a monster to all people even to them. They continue to make more V.V.'s just to get them food while the scammers on Earth are only out for money. They don't care about the facts, and they've lost count of exactly how many V.V.'s are living on Earth. Once the V.V.'s are able to live alone, they easily blend in with people and can't be distinguished. The V.V.'s are constantly killing in more numbers, not just because there is so many of them, but because they have new victims who don't even know what A.V.T.A. is. Some try hugs, kisses, pushing, and punching but once that V.V. is touched more than three times, it will kill that person and go on living as if it was a real person making it able to seek more victims because it walks amongst people everywhere at all times. So many scammers just don't agree with each other and they try to run the V.V.'s against each other but that never works. That causes a V.V. to immediately multiply five times their already high number. Out of those five, only two of them can face Judge Butler. The other three are untouchable. Even the scammers that created it can't do anything about it. The big ploys by the scammers have really backfired on them.

The judge has to decide another extremely delicate case that he can't handle. It's a few days after he had fell down shouting "no" as he was shrinking his power. The case is again, similar to his own except this V.V. is a lady. Now don't forget that V.V.'s do not have any feelings at all. This V.V. looks exactly like a younger version of his mother, whom he'd killed. Judge Butler is absolutely speechless and sweating alot. He'd never been seen sweating before. He begans to shout "No!" The V.V. just stands in front of him, looking into his eyes. It's almost as if she is grinning and wanting to laugh at him but a V.V. doesn't display any emotion, good or bad. She just waits until one of the scammers that created her will press the buttons and then send her to a new victim. Judge Butler then falls down again still shouting "No!" This time he's sweating and the officers who assist him are very nervous. They panic and also shout "No!" with him. They realize that there's really no hope without a judge with his strength and A.V.T.A. will increase even faster and the number of people murdered will triple in a few weeks. The officers are desperate because there's also a high number of officers who are A.V.T.A. customers. As the judge starts to shrink, he continues to look into the eyes of the female

V.V. and she doesn't stop looking into his eyes as she has a very deceitful look on her face. The scammers everywhere began celebrating and laughing very loud. The officers are lost and anxious to see the judge stand up strongly again as he's shrinking in size and sweating alot. The officers released the V.V. from the court room. She quickly vanishes and focuses on the next people to deceive and destroy. Officers and millions of people start to cry and scream "No, no, help us!" As they looked up into the sky. When the judge looked up into the sky, rain starts pouring down everywhere. Then, thunder strikes twice, each time the word "Love", is heard from the sky. Everyone is hearing it and looking at each other. Then, the third strike hits the judge. Many people lose their breath. He rises to his feet and then continues on to the next V.V. case he must decide.

It's almost like the judge didn't realize what had just happened. He's not sweating but he's smaller than before. Worldwide, people start to say "Love, love!" to each other. The majority of the scammers began to settle their differences with each other because they feel that they really have the upper hand now seeing how short and thin the judge is now. Even though that female V.V. is nowhere to be found by anyone, the scammers have the ability to quickly and easily create another one. Even though Judge Butler was originally created by them, they don't want to believe that he is now powered by love and God will not let them control him again. Love is mighty.

The scammers do not believe in God anyway. The ones who live on the new planet actually are thinking that they rule the universe and continue the A.V.T.A. assault on mankind. They also don't realize that Judge Butler will never perish as long as there's a small drop on love left on Earth. Even if the love remaining is smaller than a tear drop, Judge Butler can remain.

If there is no love on Earth, then Earth shouldn't exist anymore. The scammers are very convinced that this new planet will be the future for life. For a new beginning, and they want to keep getting wealthy so they can rule.

The biggest concern of the scammers is getting rich. The ones on the new planet focus more on having food brought to them. As much as possible. The scammers who are still on Earth focus on going to the new planet and leaving Earth behind. That's why they work together alot more and more often.

God is ruler of all. God is king of the universe. A new planet doesn't mean a thing without any love there. The scammers have totally forgotten what love is, just like so many A.V.T.A. customers have forgotten about reality. Hurt, lust, and hopeless.

So many people have put their religions aside and that shows how evil A.V.T.A. really is. For so many to actually make their religions secondary to the temporary satisfaction of A.V.T.A. and the scammers enjoy this, and continue to build, love is desperately needed. God isn't worried about A.V.T.A. he just wants people to love. He can erase A.V.T.A. with one drop of rain or one tear. For people to easily forget about him and decades of studying many religions, God doesn't feel mad, but he feels betrayed. Where is the love? People aren't wise enough to actually feel that A.V.T.A. is satan's newest weapon. They'll never stop their belief in their religions and faith in God. Never stop having hope no matter what.

All who have love, will be blessed. Living on any planet is minor when compared to living in heaven. So many don't want to see Earth be destroyed because of all of the wonderful memories and so many of their loved ones are buried in their graves on Earth. No one knows the exact number of who will make it to heaven, like scammers do not know the exact number of V.V.'s because it is far too many. They even know the exact number of people that they've killed with A.V.T.A. because they constantly celebrate with each other at any time, day or night.

A.V.T.A. is the world's biggest foe ever (besides the devil of course). Mostly everybody really do feel that the end of the world has finally come.

For people to be able to notice when the last days are upon them, it gives them enough time to get righteous. Many will clean up their acts and spread more love everywhere. The expansion of love will slowly, but for surely, increase the power of Judge Butler. His size slowly increases too, but nobody notices that. The officers who witnessed both V.V.'s that weakened the judge, have difficulty remembering how their appearances. Judge Butler has so many cases at one time and he was also created by the scammers and those are two more limits for him. The world simply - must help him in everyway possible. Just like he's been so helpful. People must believe in their love and make peace for everyone. When the-love-is-stronger, A.V.T.A. will fall forever. The scammers who remain on Earth will face punishment immediately. The ones in space on that new planet will perish and no one will remember them. When the scammers are gone, the V.V.'s will disappear. Earth still wouldn't be the perfect place but as long as everyone is aware of the power of having love, things will be alot easier.

Being hurt and the pain of losing someone that you've had alot of love for is always going to remain. There will always be tests that-we-must-encounter. We have to be doing what is right. There must always be hope and trust in God. To have a virtual version of someone that is so close to you, be allowed to kill, is really terror. We all must understand life and what is true.

War, disease, deception for money, and impatience all hit Earth hard each time. A.V.T.A. hit just as hard also. Scammers always knew that what they'd built was totally out of order. They were blinded by greed always.

Alot of punishment continued. Many people still pursued A.V.T.A. They didn't want to except not having that access that A.V.T.A. provided, though expensive, short periods of time, and really careless. An extremely large number of A.V.T.A. customers would become computer technologists and scammers themselves just to keep their V.V.'s ongoing. Losing the same love twice is very devastating. Many are already battling physical, mental, and family problems. Just to purchase A.V.T.A. would already display a major weakness and totally being unstable. The scammers liked to take advantage of so many people in need. The scammers would take advantage of each other because they were also without trust. All of the money and relocating to a new planet only backfired on them. That's what is known as charma.

Judge Butler continued to do his job through the rougher times. The numbers of murder and suicides by previous A.V.T.A. customers would increase. Still with numbers of new cases before him most of the time, he knew that there's still a big shortage of love everywhere. He kept some kind of authority over the V.V.'s and the scammers with their A.V.T.A. contracts, only he could slow down the madness. He gave hope again to the children victims of A.V.T.A.

Many judges and other law officials watched Judge Butler very closely. Tryin to figure him out. Constantly trying to learn from him. They only picked-up on his calmness. Judge Butler remains calm because he has hope. He really regrets what he had done to his own parents and it only shows that A.V.T.A. is no match for real love.

Judge Butler was still facing similar cases to his own. He was weakened but he prevailed because the number of scammers had decreased. There was still a large amount of V.V.'s and the smaller number of scammers really didn't have control anymore. Many of the remaining V.V.'s live alone. Very numerous and still on the prowl. The remaining V.V.'s were almost undetectable. They would not have to face Judge Butler or any justice because they don't have contracts or scammers to deal with. Once they're connected back to any scammer, it can vanish and get away unpunished. The number of remaining V.V.'s to Judge Butler is approximately 10,000 to one. There's roughly three thousand scammers left. Alot of people who want A.V.T.A. to remain desperately learn from scammers and that gives the scammers alot of their control back. Things aren't as tough because people are finally coming back to reality. The love is stronger. Judge Butler has influenced so many people and they're very thankful for all that he has done. Law enforcement has improved, everyone has alot more hope.

The judicial system is finally coming down harder than before on the scammers. Large numbers of them have to work with law enforcement or else they'll face life sentences when caught.

With the scammers cooperating and people are realizing that A.V.T.A. is not true at all. The V.V.'s that are uncontrolled by the scammers will eventually destroy each other because they are without guidance and repeat the same steps. They will disappear when the stronger law and scammers helping and teaching all of the tricks and trades just so they can be released one day. The jails are designed with computers now, to be only used by scammers who can help control things while incarcerated. There were many different opinions of having computers for the scammers doing time, but they are needed so much. It makes things easier even though there are many guards at the jails who support A.V.T.A. so things aren't solid. Prisoners are learning from the scammers and get free and just uplift the A.V.T.A. mahem without that access to a new planet, seeming invincible. More and more of the scammers realize that they can't win against what is right. They are only given two options, life in jail or a death sentence and on top of that, their numbers were decreasing. Most of the scammers are sentenced to death or they will have to work with law enforcement for the rest of their lives. A large number of the scammers already didn't trust each other. Alot of envy and no loyalty. The computers in the jails are very risky, but they become a major weapon against A.V.T.A. though there are flaws. It's almost as if the scammers in jail work harder than the ones free because they are on close watch and their lives are on the line. The prisoners who learn from the scammers also help against A.V.T.A. so that they can get their sentences reduced. Putting the computers there was expensive but it became a major weapon. After the V.V.'s and scammers go before Judge Butler, the V.V.'s are incarcerated for a few days or less until another scammer takes control of it. With the actions of the judge, wiser people, and actually having prisoners help out, things slowly get better. The entire A.V.T.A. operation is slowed down but not completely gone because of its supporters and the world still needs more love. People are still highly effected by losing a loved one and continue basically fooling themselves by forgetting about what is for real.

Once the world finally had more defense against A.V.T.A. after seven years, Judge Butler gets struck by lightning and then he vanished. Not many people notice what had happened. With the decrease of V.V.'s and help from jails, it seemed that most people didn't really depend or look to the judge for justice. Many people were somewhat satisfied with the large numbers of scammers incarcerated and their assistance. The scammers that are helping fight A.V.T.A. would become the biggest weapon for the world. Of course the judge is always needed but everyone slowly didn't pay as much attention to him. After vanishing, he would be forgiven for what he'd done to his parents and no one ever sees him again.

Sadly, the lack of love continues in the world. The A.V.T.A. victims would still continue. Without having Judge Butler's help, everyone depends on the "reformed" scammers assistance. So many prisoners and the scammers working with each other wasn't always helpful. There is also still many V.V.'s loose and unable to be detected by scammers for years, even though there's more defense against A.V.T.A. continues until there is more love everywhere. A.V.T.A. will remain an enemy. Will the world ever be right? We hope so.

Printed in the United States
by Baker & Taylor Publisher Services